Devils' Pass is published by Stone Arch Books, a Capstone Imprint
1710 Roe Crest Drive
North Mankato, Minnesota 56003
www.mycapstone.com

Text © 2018 Stone Arch Books
Illustrations © 2018 Stone Arch Books

Library of Congress Cataloging-in-Publication Data is available on the Library of Congress website.

ISBN: 978-1-4965-4987-7 (hardcover)
ISBN: 978-1-4965-4991-4 (ebook pdf)

Summary: After Tiffany Donovan tries out a new bakery for her school's annual cookie sale, she soon finds out that the cookies are more than just delicious. Per usual in Devils' Pass, things aren't what they seem. Tiffany has to join her friends and use her smarts to save the town once again.

Editor: Megan Atwood
Designer: Hilary Wacholz

Printed and bound in Canada.
010382F17

DEVILS' PASS

TIFFANY DONOVAN
VS.
THE COOKIE ELVES OF DESTRUCTION

BY JUSTINA IRELAND
ILLUSTRATED BY TYLER CHAMPION

STONE ARCH BOOKS
a capstone imprint

THE LOYAL ORDER OF HELGA

Long, long ago, in a village called New Svalbard, the people who lived there faced unimaginable dangers. A sinkhole as old as time held a door – a portal – to the Otherside, a dark and dreadful place filled with literal nightmares.

To warn travelers of the danger the village posed, the people renamed it Devils' Pass – a reminder to all who lived there and passed through that a darkness sat in the area. A darkness that often had teeth.

For years the people of Devils' Pass endured the danger. Then Helga, one of the white settlers of the village, fell through the cursed sinkhole to the Otherside, coming face-to-face with the terrifying monsters. Helga spent many years there, fighting all sorts of monstrous creatures, learning about their ways and their weaknesses. Through trials and tribulations, and more than a little cunning, she became a fearsome warrior.

Helga fought her way back to Devils' Pass through the portal, now with an understanding of the deadly secrets of the Otherside. Almost immediately, her skills were put to the test. A fearsome frost giant menaced the village, crawling out of the sinkhole and terrorizing the people. Using only a flaming torch, Helga fought the giant and won. It was an astonishing act of bravery – but soon it was clear that the people of Devils' Pass suffered from something else. The sinkhole made the people of the village forget that monsters lived there.

Through some type of magic, however, not all of them forgot. Those who remembered the perils and nightmares the sinkhole brought forth became the Loyal Order of Helga. Along with Helga, the people who remembered the danger vowed to protect Devils' Pass – and the entire world – from the vicious monsters of the Otherside.

CHAPTER ONE
A Strange Donation

Monday morning, Tiffany Donovan ran out of the house thirty minutes earlier than usual. It was the day of the annual Devils' Pass Middle School Cookie Sale. As student body president, it was Tiffany's job to make sure there were plenty of cookies for people to buy. This meant that she had to get up earlier and leave without breakfast. Tiffany hated missing breakfast and hated being late to school. Not to mention, cookies were not an excuse for tardiness.

It was her fault she had to buy cookies in the first place. Yesterday, while baking cookies for the sale, she'd gotten distracted by the show *Gem War Attack*, her friend Zach Lopez's favorite show. She'd promised Zach she would watch the show and then discuss it with him. But she'd also promised to bake cookies for the sale and work on the group project for her science class. Plus, she still had to make time to practice for soccer tryouts next month, so she'd been dribbling a soccer ball on her knees while cutting and pasting diagrams for class and watching *Gem War Attack*.

She ended up accidentally cutting one of the diagrams in half. Then she missed most of the show when she lost control of the soccer ball and it knocked over her water bottle. The cookies burned and she missed the rest of the show, and the group project still wasn't finished. It had been a totally wasted day.

And now here she was trying to make up time by hurrying to the Devils' Pass Bakery before the sun was even up. She tried never to walk outside when it was dark. Not in Devils' Pass, anyway.

As she jogged toward Main Street, dread filled Tiffany and made her stomach hurt. This early, Devils'

Pass looked nothing like the town Tiffany knew. All the shops were closed and no one was around. It was still dark out and the streetlights didn't do much to penetrate the gloom. A cold wind blew, stirring up dead leaves. Far off, a dog howled.

As she passed the park, Tiffany quickened her pace. Deep in the park was a sinkhole filled with inky black water. But it wasn't really a sinkhole. It was a doorway to the Otherside, a creepy world filled with monstrous unicorns and cat-eating mermaids. Every once in a while, the monsters from the Otherside made their way to Devils' Pass. Tiffany and her friends foiled their plots with the help of the town librarian, Mr. Hofstrom. As the Loyal Order of Helga, it was their job to keep the town safe from monsters, and they were good at it. But she didn't have her friends with her right now, and she didn't want to meet any of those monsters.

Once she was past the park, Tiffany's fear melted away and she began to worry about smaller things. What if the bakery wasn't open this early? Or what if they didn't have any cookies for the sale? She was

the eighth-grade class president. If she didn't bring anything to the sale, she would let everyone down.

That was not going to happen.

Main Street looked normal, the town's single stoplight blinking yellow. Tiffany sighed with relief when she saw the light pouring out of a storefront about halfway down the block. That had to be the bakery — the only place open this early.

The bakery was painted bright pink. A sign proclaimed "Cookies and More!" Inside, an older white woman whom Tiffany didn't recognize stared out from behind a counter. Tiffany frowned. There were no hours posted on the door, but since the lights were on, she figured the bakery was open.

She pulled open the door and chimes rang. As they did, the woman behind the counter turned to look at her, but in a slow and strange way. A smile was planted oddly on the woman's face.

"Good. Morning." The woman's voice sounded like the voice on a robocall. She seemed to barely register Tiffany's presence. And since Tiffany was over six feet tall with Afro puffs and dark skin, she was used to people noticing her. It felt strange to be ignored. Stranger still, Tiffany had never seen this woman before.

"Um, hi, good morning. Where's Mrs. Briggs?" Mrs. Briggs had owned the bakery since Tiffany was small. If she wanted to stock the bake sale with amazing cookies everyone would love, Mrs. Briggs was the person to make them. Her baking was legendary. "I wanted to buy some cookies?"

The woman kept smiling. "Everything is free right now. Free samples."

"Uh, and Mrs. Briggs is OK with that?" Tiffany asked, eyebrows furrowed. She seriously doubted that.

"New management!" said the woman.

"What happened to Mrs. Briggs?" Tiffany frowned. She went to school with Mason Briggs, and as far as she knew, they had no plans to move. Mrs. Briggs wouldn't sell the bakery. No way.

"The Mrs. Briggs is happy to let the bakery be managed by us. New recipes! You try our cookies and you love them," the woman said.

Tiffany shifted on her feet. The lady was odd and her speech was weird. But then Tiffany thought about when she was little and Mrs. Kostyloff moved in next door. Mrs. Kostyloff was friendly and always smiling, but she brought over foods like beet soup. Tiffany had complained to her grandma about how the lady talked funny and her food was weird. Grandma had told her, "That woman moved to the United States from Russia and learned English, which is one of the most difficult languages to learn. Do you know how to speak Russian? No? Then maybe you shouldn't make judgments about how people talk."

What if the woman behind the counter had learned English as a second language like Mrs. Kostyloff? Tiffany didn't want to be rude and ignorant.

"OK, I'd love to try your cookies, but I need, like, a hundred cookies for a sale at my school," she said, making a decision to go ahead.

"We love sales. Have our free cookies. Totally free. Very delicious. Cookies for everyone." The woman was still smiling. Tiffany scratched the back of her neck nervously.

"Um, OK. Yeah, like a donation. I'd be happy to take whatever you have." It still seemed strange to Tiffany that the woman wanted to give away her cookies, but what better advertising than giving cookies to the middle school? Plus, Tiffany was running out of time. She had to get to school. And she really needed those cookies for the sale.

The woman turned around and walked to a door, entering a back room. Tiffany looked around the shop while she waited. The cases were empty. When Mrs. Briggs was there, the cases had cakes and pastries and pies for customers to see. But not anymore. She made a mental note to ask her grandma what had happened to Mrs. Briggs.

The woman came back with a huge tray covered with cookies. "Donation," she said, offering the cookies to Tiffany.

"Um, thanks. Do you want me to tell folks about your cookies or anything?" Tiffany asked.

The woman nodded, still smiling. She avoided Tiffany's eyes, which seemed like an odd thing to do. But maybe it was a cultural thing? She nodded again and her wig slipped forward a little. Tiffany looked away in embarrassment. The woman didn't seem to notice that her hair was sliding down over her eyes. "Yes. Free cookies. All this week," she said.

"OK. Thanks again." Tiffany backed out of the shop with the huge tray of cookies, the woman smiling all the while, her wig slightly askew. Back on the sidewalk, Tiffany took in a deep breath and then let it out.

Suddenly, Main Street didn't seem so creepy after the weirdness in the bakery.

Still, Tiffany hurried the rest of the way to school, the feeling of being watched prickling the back of her neck all the way there.

CHAPTER TWO
Some Smart Cookies

Tiffany got to school with a little time to spare
before the first bell rang. She dropped off her cookies
at the bake sale table and went to the library to study
for a math test before classes started. But on the
way there, she ran into her friends. Zach Lopez was
standing with Jeff and Evie Allen, Tiffany's other best
friends. Together, the four of them were the Loyal
Order of Helga. The rest of the town always forgot
about the monster attacks, thanks to a phenomenon

Tiffany had dubbed "goldfish memory." So the Loyal Order of Helga could only depend on themselves and Mr. Hofstrom.

"Tiffany! Did you bring that book I wanted?" Evie asked.

Tiffany nodded, but then stopped. "Shoot, I think I forgot it. I had it sitting on my dresser and then was so focused on getting cookies for the cookie sale that I left it at home."

Evie's face fell a little, but she covered her disappointment with a smile. "It's OK. Could you bring it tomorrow?"

"Definitely."

"Where are you going?" Jeff asked. "I thought you were going to eat breakfast with us this morning."

"I can't," Tiffany said, even though her stomach growled. "I have a math test this morning and I—" The first bell rang, cutting her off. It had taken her more time to stop and get the cookies than she'd thought.

"Darn it! I wanted to study before my test!"

"Good luck on your test, Tiff. Oh, did you see the new episode of *Gem War Attack* last night? So good, right?" Zach asked.

Tiffany nodded and said, "Yep!" but turned and hurried to her math class. No time to talk. Her class was at the other end of the school. If she hustled, maybe she could still get there before the late bell.

Just as Tiffany slid into her seat, the bell rang and her math teacher, Ms. Collins, walked in. "Please put everything away and pull out a pencil for our test. I hope you studied!"

Tiffany groaned along with everyone else.

The rest of the morning passed in a blur. Tiffany didn't have much time to think about the cookie sale or the strange bakery lady.

But during English, Alicia Arnold, the most popular girl in school, leaned over and said, "Those cookies you brought were ah-may-zing." She pushed her blond hair behind her ear and leaned in close. "Can I get the recipe? I want to make them for the field hockey bake sale."

"I got them at the bakery on Main Street," Tiffany said. Usually the only time Alicia talked to her was when she wanted to copy homework.

Alicia nodded. "Oh, I'm going to swing by after school then. They were so good."

Lots of other people came up to ask Tiffany about the cookies, and it seemed like they were the only thing people could talk about all morning. By the time she went by the bake sale table at lunch to check on her cookies, they were all gone.

"Hey, everyone loves your cookies," Evie said. Evie was smaller than everyone else in eighth grade because she'd skipped a grade. Today she wore a shirt with a panda bear pattern and her pale skin was flushed because she had gym right before lunch.

"I noticed. They're already gone! Did you have any?" Tiffany asked.

Evie shook her head. "I didn't think they were vegan, so I decided to skip them. But Jeff had, like, six. It's the most I've seen him eat since his chemo."

The year before, Evie's brother Jeff had gotten a cancer in his leg called Ewing's sarcoma. He'd had chemotherapy, which had made him nauseated and ruined his appetite, so he didn't eat much. For him to eat so many cookies was amazing.

"I only had four. Hey, Tiff." Jeff came up, his crutches clicking on the hallway floor. Because of the cancer, Jeff had had an operation called a rotationplasty. The doctor had reconnected his foot backwards to where his knee would have been, so that a good portion of his leg was missing. The surgery allowed for better movement in a prosthetic leg, which he'd just recently gotten. But he still mostly skipped the prosthesis and used his crutches until he could get used to the leg.

"Hey. Lunch?" Tiffany asked. She was always hungry, but today was chili mac, her second-favorite school lunch, so she couldn't wait.

"Zach wanted us to wait for him by the bake sale table," Jeff said.

"I wanted to get more cookies. Dang! They're all gone," Zach said as he came running up. Zach Lopez was the newest kid at Devils' Pass Middle School. He'd just started, and his mom was the school principal. Zach had brown skin and floppy black hair, and even though Tiffany had never said anything, she thought he was really cute. Plus, he was the only Puerto Rican kid in school, and since Tiffany was the only black kid, they had a lot in common. They both knew what it felt like to be treated differently because of their skin.

"You can get some more at the bakery," Tiffany said. "The lady there was kind of weird, but she said they'd have free samples all week." Tiffany looked once more at the empty cookie tray and sighed. She'd been looking forward to having a cookie, but now they were all gone. Maybe she could stop by later and get some from the bakery. Free cookies were a great deal, especially if they were as good as everyone said they were.

"Awesome," Zach said.

"Let's go eat. I'm starving," Tiffany said.

During lunch, everyone kept stopping by the table to tell Tiffany how amazing her cookies had been. The sale was a success, thanks to her cookies in particular.

By the time lunch was over, she couldn't stop smiling.

Finally, something was going right.

CHAPTER THREE
A Bad Sign

The next day, Tiffany ran to school. She'd overslept, her alarm not even waking her up. Maybe it was because she'd stayed up late finishing her English paper, a paper she should've written a week ago — but she and her friends had been busy fighting a herd of evil unicorns. Or maybe she was late because she'd slept horribly. Tiffany had spent all night tossing and turning. She'd had a nightmare that she was making cookies over and over again, only for people to show up and eat all of them. No matter how many cookies she made, it was never enough.

Thank goodness the cookie sale was over.

Since she was running late, Tiffany decided to take a shortcut to school. The shortcut went through the park and by the sinkhole, which was why she rarely took it. Knowing that there were monsters that could pop out of the water at any time made Tiffany nervous, and the park was usually empty in the morning. Even though there was a chain-link fence around the sinkhole, that wasn't usually enough to keep the monsters out of the park. If Tiffany had to face down Otherside creatures, she didn't want to do it by herself.

But today she was more concerned with being on time than whatever creepiness existed in the park. And there was plenty of creepiness.

Tiffany ran, the cold morning air making her eyes water. It was only November, but there was already frost on the cars and a few errant snowflakes danced through the air. She ducked her head into the collar of her sweatshirt, wishing she'd thought to wear her coat. She wasn't paying attention to where she was going, which is why she ran right into the bakery lady, who was carrying a tray of cookies.

"Oof!" Tiffany stumbled backward, but managed to stay on her feet. The bakery lady was not so lucky, and she landed hard on her rear end. The cookies flew off the tray, scattering all over the park path. Tiffany saw that the lady's wig now tilted precariously to the right.

"I am so, so sorry!" Tiffany exclaimed. "I wasn't paying attention to where I was going."

The woman smiled wide and stared vacantly at Tiffany. "Would you like a cookie?" She didn't seem to notice that all the cookies from her tray had fallen onto the ground or that her wig was about to fall off.

Tiffany caught a glimpse of her scalp under the wig. She could see strange red marks all over. They looked like tiny teeth marks, almost like someone had eaten her hair and bitten her scalp while they were at it.

Tiffany took a step back, and raised her hands. "No, I think I'm good. Are you OK?"

"The cookies are free. Have one." The woman was still smiling. She sat in the middle of the path, oblivious to everything except offering Tiffany one of

her cookies. Tiffany noticed that the cookies were very quickly melting into the path.

A terrible feeling washed over her, like the time she'd accidentally washed her sister's cashmere sweater in hot water and shrunk it down to doll size. There was definitely something wrong with the cookie woman. Maybe she had hit her head when she fell? But that didn't explain those weird teeth marks on her scalp. Those had to come from something else. Something Otherside.

This seemed like a monster emergency.

But first things first: Tiffany had to get the woman some medical help.

"Hey, I'm going to go get some help. Stay right here, OK?" The woman didn't seem to hear Tiffany, and she didn't wait for her to agree. Tiffany ran down the path and onto Main Street. The police station was at the end of the street, and one of the officers would be able to call an ambulance for the woman.

Tiffany ran out of the park and skidded to a stop.

There was a crowd of people in front of the bakery, the line nearly around the block. Teachers and kids from school made up most of the crowd, but Tiffany also saw folks like Officer Arnold, Alicia Arnold's dad. Instead of heading to the police station, Tiffany ran straight to the line spilling out of the bakery.

"Officer Arnold! I think there's an old woman hurt in the park," Tiffany said, gasping for breath.

Officer Arnold scowled. "I'm waiting in line for cookies, Tiffany."

"I know sir, but she's really hurt. Confused and disoriented. She might have a concussion." She didn't mention the tiny bite marks. That was a question for Mr. Hofstrom, not the police officer. And probably a doctor.

Officer Arnold sighed. "Show me where this woman is."

Tiffany led the way back through the park. She tried to rush, but Officer Arnold wasn't interested in running. They walked briskly instead. Tiffany was taller than the police officer — she was taller than just about everyone — and several times he told her to wait up. By the time they arrived at the spot in the path where the lady had fallen, both Tiffany and Officer Arnold were irritated and out of sorts.

"Where is she?" Officer Arnold asked when Tiffany stopped. She looked around the path and the grass, but there was no woman. She had disappeared. The tray the cookies had been on was alongside the path, but there were no signs of the woman or any cookies anywhere.

"She was right here," Tiffany said. Her panic was starting to fade away, leaving confusion in its place. "I know she was right here."

"Well, she isn't here now. Looks like she was just fine. You'd better hope they don't run out of chocolate chip cookies before I get some, Miss Donovan," he said, his voice gruff. He didn't wait for Tiffany's response before he walked off, moving much faster back to the bakery than he had walked to the park.

Tiffany looked around at the path, but there was no sign of the woman or the cookies anywhere. Instead, all she saw was the empty cookie tray and tufts of what looked like dryer lint all over the path.

Tiffany couldn't help but glance toward the back of the park and the dark waters of the sinkhole. She could just barely see it from here.

She was beginning to get the feeling that there was a reason everyone had loved her cookies. And she was certain that the reason had to be bad.

CHAPTER FOUR
Business Is Booming

After her disastrous morning, the rest of Tiffany's day was uneventful. When she met up with Jeff, Zach, and Evie after school, the weird cookie-pushing lady was the first thing she had to talk about. Those tiny bites had been gross, and there definitely had to be some kind of monster running around Devils' Pass. If they acted quickly, maybe they could save the town before any more people were hurt like the cookie lady had been. Tiffany was worried that whatever had been chewing on her head might have finished her off that morning in the park.

So when Tiffany saw the cookie lady standing in the parking lot after school talking to Zach's mom, Principal Lopez, she yelped in surprise.

"What's wrong?" Evie asked.

Tiffany quickly explained about running into the lady in the park and her weird behavior, as well as the bite marks on her head. "Officer Arnold was so mad at me. All he cared about was getting back to the bakery to eat the cookies."

"That's because those cookies rock," Jeff said. "Besides, she looks OK to me. Nothing seemed to have happened. She was just probably not listening to you when you were talking."

Zach nodded in agreement. "Yeah, my mom does that sometimes when she's thinking about other stuff. It's totally normal."

"Tiffany said she had bite marks all over her head, Zach," Evie said, her voice filled with disbelief.

Jeff shrugged. "You said that she was wearing a wig. Maybe she just had some sort of allergic reaction."

Tiffany pressed her lips together. Nothing about the way the woman had acted seemed normal. And now, Jeff and Zach were also acting weird. Both of them usually believed her when she said something, but now they were acting like she was making up the whole mess in the park. Why were they acting like such jerks?

She looked at Evie, but Evie just shrugged. Tiffany turned her attention back to the cookie lady and Principal Lopez. They finished chatting, and when the woman left, Tiffany headed straight over to the principal. Zach, Evie, and Jeff followed closely behind.

Tiffany focused on Ms. Lopez. She'd find out what was going on by herself if she had to.

"Hi, Principal Lopez!" Tiffany said brightly, turning on what she called her "grown-up" voice. Whenever she spoke to adults, it was helpful to sound happy and excited about things. There was a reason she'd been teacher's pet since fourth grade.

Principal Lopez smiled at Tiffany. "How are we doing today, Ms. Donovan?"

"Very well, ma'am," she answered. Behind her, she could hear Zach ask Jeff and Evie, "Why is she talking like that?" but she ignored him and continued.

"I couldn't help but see that you were talking to the woman from Cookies and More, Ms. Lopez. I was just wondering if there was any specific reason for that?" Tiffany asked.

Principal Lopez laughed and crossed her arms. "Well, there is. I was going to save it as a surprise to announce to the entire school, but since you're the student body president, I suppose I can tell you first. We just signed a deal with the local bakery to give away their cookies in the cafeteria. They're a very generous company, dedicated to donating to local schools."

Tiffany blinked. "Wait, you can do that?"

Principal Lopez grinned. "Well, it is unorthodox, but I think this is a case where we can make an exception. Their cookies are phenomenal, and the bakery is a pillar of the community. See you tomorrow, Ms. Donovan. Zach, make sure you get your math homework done before I get home."

"OK, Mom," Zach said.

Principal Lopez walked away, and Evie put a hand on Tiffany's arm. "You look worried."

"I am worried. Since when do teachers want more junk food in the school cafeteria? And I know that cookie lady was hurt this morning, and now she looks fine. This is so weird. Everyone is acting like these cookies are magical," Tiffany said.

"Those cookies are magical," Jeff said. "You should have one."

"I'm sure it's all completely normal," Evie said. But she bit her lip and looked down.

"Do you really believe that?" Tiffany asked, eyeing her. This was Devils' Pass. Nothing was normal here.

Evie was quiet for a long time before she said, "Well, no one has been hurt yet, and nobody's even gone missing. So everything has to be just fine!" She forced a smile. "Besides, you've been really stressed lately, what with all your homework, the student council stuff, soccer tryouts, young science explorers…"

"Augh! I totally forgot I have a meeting after school!" Tiffany slapped her forehead and groaned. "We're supposed to be planning out our projects for the science fair. I gotta go. See you guys later."

She jogged back to school, thinking about what Evie had said. Maybe Evie was right. No one had gone missing. No one had shown up dead.

There was just the weird cookie lady.

Maybe those strange marks on the lady's head were just some sort of an allergic reaction. Maybe all this school stress was making Tiffany see monsters where there weren't any.

But of course she knew she didn't really believe that.

CHAPTER FIVE
Cookie Monster?

For the next week, the cookies from the bakery were all anyone at school could talk about. Between classes, kids ate cookies that their parents had packed in their backpacks, and the line for cookies was the longest in the cafeteria every day at lunch. It seemed that the only people not eating the cookies were Evie and Tiffany: Evie because they weren't vegan, and Tiffany because some of the cookies had nuts, which was a huge risk with her peanut allergy. If she accidentally ate a cookie full of peanuts, the possibility of cookie monsters wouldn't matter much.

And anyway, she didn't exactly trust the cookies, peanuts or not.

Zach and Jeff thought Tiffany was just overreacting about the cookies. But halfway through the week, people started getting strange marks on their arms. Marks that looked like little bites. But no one seemed to care. They only wanted more cookies. Yet another reason Tiffany wanted to stay away from them.

"You should try one," Zach said, offering one of the stack of twenty or so on his tray. They were sitting at lunch about a week after the cookie sale, and everyone was still deep in the throes of cookie fever, as Tiffany had taken to calling it. Zach usually packed his lunch, but since the cookies had appeared in the cafeteria, he'd been a buyer.

Tiffany huffed in frustration. She was in the small space next to the lunch table, trying to practice dribbling her soccer ball. She would get in trouble if any of the teachers monitoring the lunchroom saw her. No one ever noticed the lunch table of the Loyal Order of Helga, though — the unpredictable magic that protected the Order seemed to cloak it. No teachers had noticed her, but she still hated to risk it. She was so far behind on her practice schedule, she felt as if she had no choice. She tried one more move but lost control of the ball. A teacher saw it rolling on the ground and looked around, a confused look on her face.

Tiffany sighed and sat down. "I just asked if you noticed the marks on some of the students' arms? I keep seeing students with what looks like teeth marks on their arms."

Zach shrugged. "People look fine to me. Are you sure you don't want a cookie? I mean, they're really good."

"Uh, no, thanks. I have to be careful because of my peanut allergy," Tiffany said. "But we need to start investigating this cookie madness. Doesn't any of this strike anyone as strange? These cookies are most definitely monster cookies!"

"Hey, don't you have student council today?" Evie asked, her mouth full of sandwich.

"Oh no, I do, and I totally forgot to bring in the poster-making supplies!" Tiffany gathered up her things and ran from the table, while Zach and Jeff munched on cookies and Evie watched them with a worried expression.

That night at home, Tiffany did an Internet search on Devils' Pass. No one was missing. No bite marks in the news. Nothing at all was strange or weird or unexplained.

Tiffany did another Internet search, this time for the entire county. And there, in an article about a missing woman from Dunsville, was the Cookie Lady.

The Cookie Lady was really named Mary Rogers, and she'd gone missing in the middle of the night. According to the article, her family was worried, too, because she'd left the house without putting on her favorite wig.

Jackpot.

Tiffany copied the link to the article and drafted an email to Zach, Jeff, and Evie. "COOKIE MONSTERS!" the subject said, and she sent it off with a self-satisfied smile.

She knew there were monsters. Now they just had to find them and stop them.

CHAPTER SIX

Situation Almost Normal. Maybe.

The next day — the day of Tiffany's triumphant assertion that yes, there was a monster in Devils' Pass — the cookies were gone.

Tiffany walked into the cafeteria expecting to see a line snaking around the perimeter, but there was no one. Instead, everyone was sitting at their normal tables eating, and the lunch lines had gone back to their pre-cookie lack-of-hysteria levels.

"Hey, Tiffany, how are you doing today, hon?" asked the lunch lady, Ms. Doris.

"Good, Ms. Doris. Where did everyone go? The line is way shorter than yesterday," Tiffany said.

Ms. Doris smiled and shrugged. "It seems that we're all out of those cookies you kids went gaga for. I couldn't have any. Have to watch my sugar, you know. But they sure did look good."

Tiffany nodded and took her tray. She couldn't help but feel a sense of relief that the cookie madness was over. For the past week, she'd worried that she might have been responsible for something really bad happening to the people of Devils' Pass. But it seemed to have ended. Maybe it really was just a trend and not a monster.

Maybe those weird marks on people's arms and the Cookie Lady's head had been a rash. Hives or something. After all, it wasn't like Tiffany was a doctor. Not yet, anyway.

Did this mean she had been wrong about cookie monsters in Devils' Pass? Could it be that Tiffany Donovan was just wrong? But what about Mary Rogers, the Cookie Lady?

She suddenly felt silly. She really had been overreacting. It must be from all the stress. Maybe her sister Simone was right. She kept telling Tiffany that she was an overachiever. "You have too many activities. You're going to end up doing a bunch of things badly instead of one or two things well. And then your hair will fall out and you'll be seven kinds of sad." Tiffany didn't really think her hair was going to fall out, but it seemed like Simone was right about Tiffany doing too much.

Being stressed had her seeing monsters where there weren't any. Mary Rogers must be a totally different person than the Cookie Lady she'd interacted with.

Tiffany sat down at the table with her friends. Zach and Jeff were arguing about the best way to beat level twenty-five in Falcon Quest, a video game they loved. Evie was studying for the science test she had after lunch. It was so normal that Tiffany had to laugh. "Hey, did you want to talk about the email you sent last night?" Evie asked. "The lady looked kind of like the lady from Cookies and More."

Tiffany shook her head. "I think I made a mistake. She's just some lady who went missing."

Evie sighed. "That's so sad," she said, before returning to her sandwich.

Cookie hysteria was really over with. Finally, things could get back to normal at Devils' Pass Middle School.

CHAPTER SEVEN

Everyone's Up in Arms

Tiffany walked to school the next day feeling better than she had in weeks.

"This is going to be a great day," she said to no one in particular. The sun was shining and it was unseasonably warm.

All was well until she got inside the school.

Tiffany headed straight to her locker. Before class she liked to read a book and eat her breakfast bar. This morning, the book was a vampire romance her sister had given her, and her breakfast bar was raspberry.

As she ate, Tiffany watched the other students of Devils' Pass Middle School enter the building. She looked up just as Mason Briggs walked past. She did a double take: his arm looked horrible, full of tiny bite marks. Tiffany stopped chewing and swallowed down the lump of breakfast bar.

She caught up to him and stopped him in the hall. "Mason, what happened to your arm? Do you need some help?" The wounds wept a clear, pink-tinged liquid, and every few seconds, a droplet would hit the floor. "You need to go to the nurse's office now," she said.

Mason looked at his arm and shrugged. "Calm down, Tiffany. It's just a scrape."

"That is not a scrape!" Tiffany yelled. The more she looked at Mason's arm, the grosser it looked. No one else seemed to notice.

All of the happiness Tiffany had felt on the way to school disappeared. There had to be some type of cookie monster in town, otherwise she wouldn't be the only one freaking out about Mason's arm.

Mason looked at his badly chewed arm and then looked back at Tiffany. "It's not that bad," he said, his voice flat and toneless. It reminded Tiffany of something but she couldn't put her finger on it. He went on, "Just a bit of a rash."

"That isn't a rash, Mason. You need to go see the nurse." Tiffany held her hand over her mouth. Mason always smelled a little off; it was well-known throughout school that he thought showers were a waste of time. But today he was a level of stink that Tiffany had never smelled before, like rotten cheese crossed with hot farts.

"You have to get your arm looked at," Tiffany said. "I think it's infected." She had to get him to the nurse's office. At least then she could figure out what had attacked him. Doom unicorns? Zombies? Only a monster attack could cause that much damage and also leave Mason completely unconcerned about it.

Tiffany couldn't believe that no one else noticed Mason's arm. Her classmates moved through the hall with shuffling feet, heads down.

Mason smiled at her, his eyes looking at something over her left shoulder instead of at her. "I'm fine, everything is great. Have a nice day, Tiffany Donovan," he said as he walked away.

And then Tiffany knew exactly what he sounded like: a robot.

Just like the Cookie Lady.

Tiffany groaned. There were monsters in Devils' Pass. Of course. Her short-lived delusion that all was OK was gone. It was time to find out what the monsters were and what they were after.

CHAPTER EIGHT

School's a Snore

In her first period class, the teacher had them watch a movie instead of doing a lesson. The movie was on some famous mathematician, but Tiffany couldn't pay any attention to it. She was too distracted by the memory of Mason's arm, and how much it had looked like a worse version of what she'd seen on the Cookie Lady's bare scalp. Plus, both he and the Cookie Lady had talked in a weird sort of monotone. It was definitely an Otherside monster — but what kind of monster made people eat cookies? And then ate the people?

An evil witch à la Hansel and Gretel?

People-eating gingerbread men?

Tiffany began making a list of possible monsters and another list of symptoms to ask Mr. Hofstrom about, but she was distracted by the sound of Alicia Arnold snoring loudly next to her.

"Alicia. Alicia!" Tiffany shook her shoulder.

"Huh, what?" Alicia startled awake, and Tiffany sighed.

"You were snoring so loudly, I couldn't hear the movie," Tiffany whispered. It wasn't like she could tell Alicia about the possible monster list. She would think Tiffany was a weirdo.

Alicia yawned, covering her mouth as she did. "I'm so sorry, Tiff. I've just been sleeping really terribly, you know? We have a game this Saturday and I'm super worried I'm going to end up sleeping on the field. I went to bed at six last night and still woke up tired."

Tiffany didn't say anything, but now that Alicia had mentioned it, she couldn't help but notice that nearly everyone in the class was half asleep. Even the math teacher, Ms. Krall, looked as though she could barely keep her eyes open.

Tiffany pursed her lips in dismay. It wasn't as bad as Mason's arm, but it definitely seemed weird. She leaned over to try to get a glimpse of Alicia's arm, but she wore long sleeves and there was no way to tell if she had the same bite marks as Mason.

Tiffany wrote "makes people sleepy" and "takes tiny bites" to her list of symptoms.

The bell rang. Tiffany set out to find her friends and get the Loyal Order of Helga on the case.

CHAPTER NINE

Open for Business! Kind of.

"So, what, you think the cookies are stealing everyone's sleep or something?" Evie asked. She and Tiffany were sitting in the cafeteria waiting for Jeff and Zach. Tiffany told Evie how that morning everyone in her math class had been half asleep, and a few folks had tiny marks on their arms. But it hadn't just been her math class. In all of her classes all morning, everyone was really super tired.

"I don't know," Tiffany said. "People being sleepy seems like the less bad thing right now. I mean, Mason's arm was really gross."

Evie sighed. "Mason is always gross. Remember that time he spilled mustard on his shirt and then wore the same shirt the next day? It's probably just him being him. But you said he sounded like a robot too?"

Tiffany poked at her ham loaf, her least favorite school lunch. She nodded. "Yeah, it was weird. He was way out of it. Maybe he was sleepy like everyone else? And then his arm. . . . What were your classes like? Did everyone seem super tired and out of it to you too?" she asked Evie.

Evie nodded, taking a bite of her avocado sandwich. "Yeah, most definitely. We played dodgeball and I pegged Chad Hansen in the head three times. He barely even noticed." Chad Hansen was a dodgeball legend at Devils' Pass Middle School. He'd once gone three months never getting out in dodgeball, and he had an arm like a cannon. Most kids hated facing off against him.

"Wow," Tiffany said. "That does seem like the drowsiness is somehow tied to the cookies. Especially since I don't feel tired, and I didn't have any."

"Exactly. I don't feel tired, either," Evie said. "Why don't we ask the boys how they're feeling when they get here? They both ate a bunch of those cookies."

Tiffany's face fell when she saw Zach and Jeff head toward their table. Jeff was using his crutches again instead of wearing his prosthesis. Zach was carrying Jeff's tray for him, since it was difficult for Jeff to navigate with his crutches and carry a tray. But both of the boys looked like they hadn't slept in a while, and now Tiffany knew for sure that the cookies were somehow to blame.

"Hey," Jeff said, sitting down next to Tiffany.

"Hey. Where's your new leg? I thought you were going to wear it," she said. Jeff had waited since last spring to get a prosthetic leg that fit well, and last week he'd picked it up. Tiffany thought it was cool that Jeff would be able to walk with a prosthetic leg now.

Jeff did not think it was so cool.

He made a face. "Next week. There was a piece that needed to be replaced and it got lost in the mail."

Tiffany looked from Zach to Jeff. "You guys look tired," she said.

Zach yawned and nodded. "That's because we are. I haven't slept in, like, a week. I keep having nightmares about making cookies and someone poking me with a fork for not working fast enough."

Jeff laughed. "Oh, man, I've been having the same dream! What are the chances?"

Tiffany and Evie exchanged a look. "Actually, the chances are pretty high. We think the cookies are bad news," Evie said.

Zach frowned. "What do you mean?"

"Everyone in school is barely awake. Look, Heather Day is over there sleeping in her pudding," Tiffany said. Sure enough, the girl had fallen asleep, her spoon with pudding spilling over right next to her face on the table.

"And you think the cookies have something to do with this?" Jeff said.

"Yeah. And I think that the Cookie Lady is being controlled by whatever is doing this. And maybe she is the lady who disappeared a while back from a different town, after all. Like that article I sent you talked about," Tiffany said.

"She acted totally normal to me," Zach said. "I mean, it wasn't like she was a unicorn with shark's teeth or something."

"Tiff says she acted like a robot. That sounds fishy to me," Evie said.

"Yep," Tiffany said, tapping her chin. "We need to get into that bakery and look around."

"Cookies and More is out of business," Jeff said.

"What? Since when?" Tiffany asked.

"I don't know, a couple days ago? I went by to see if I could get some cookies and the bakery is closed. My mom told me this morning that it was for sale," Jeff said, yawning widely.

"I can't believe Mrs. Briggs sold her bakery just to have it closed down so quickly," Evie said.

"Well, maybe now she can make sure her son, Mason, showers more often," Jeff said.

"That's mean!" Evie admonished.

Tiffany smiled. "But true. Anyway, there might be some clues in the building. Maybe something that will let us know what we're up against."

Evie looked at Tiffany's tray. "You aren't eating," she said.

"I don't have much of an appetite," Tiffany confessed.

Evie bit her lip but said nothing. Jeff frowned. "You must be really worried. You never miss a meal."

Next to Jeff, Zach began to snore loudly. Tiffany and Evie giggled, and Jeff shook him awake.

"Huh, what?" Zach said.

"How are you drooling after only a couple of seconds?" Jeff asked.

Zach stretched his arms over his head. "I don't know. Oh, man, I am so tired."

Tiffany suddenly remembered to ask, "Hey, you guys don't have any marks on your arms, do you?"

"What are you talking about?" Jeff asked.

Tiffany filled in the boys on the strange bite marks on everyone's arms, and their expressions turned grim.

Both Zach and Jeff shook their heads, pulling up their sleeves to show Tiffany. She felt relieved and confused. The cookies had to be bad, but why did only some people have bite marks?

"I'm going to be so mad if I get eaten," Zach said, pulling his sleeves back down.

"We have to get into the bakery and see if there are any clues," Tiffany said, bringing the conversation back to the topic at hand.

Jeff rubbed his chin thoughtfully. "You know, my mom has extra keys for some of the shops in town — she uses them for her real estate business sometimes. I bet she has an extra key to the bakery in her office. If we borrow it from her, we could see what's going on inside. Maybe the monsters left some clues."

Evie's eyes widened. "That's stealing!"

Jeff scowled. "It's not stealing, it's borrowing. We're going to put it back. Besides, it's that or get eaten."

Tiffany nodded. "Most of the stores on Main Street close at seven. If we head down there at eight, no one should see us."

Jeff nodded. "That would be perfect. Mom usually watches *Let's Dance!* at that time. I think tonight is the pre-semi-final final. She's going to be so wrapped up in that she won't even notice we're gone."

Tiffany drank the rest of her chocolate milk and smashed the carton. "Excellent. Let's find out what's going on in this town."

CHAPTER TEN
Well, Rats.

Jeff, Zach, Tiffany, and Evie met in front of the bakery at exactly eight. The street was mostly empty and a chill wind blew a few scattered leaves in between the alleys of the buildings. They looked through the window to the bakery, but it was dark inside. Far off, a dog barked, but Main Street was eerily quiet.

"There's no lockbox here," Evie said, pointing to the front door.

"Maybe it's around back?" Jeff suggested, leaning heavily on his crutches.

"Let's go," Tiffany said, nodding.

In the back of the building there were fewer lights, and old dumpsters cast shadows onto the parking lot. Jeff and Zach walked up to the big metal door that led to the building, and Zach pointed at the door before covering his mouth as he yawned. "Let's go before I lose my nerve. Main Street is creepy after dark."

"I don't know if this is such a good idea, you guys," Evie said, hugging herself.

"We have to see if we can figure out where those cookies came from. I'm hoping we can ask Mr. Hofstom what's going on if we have some more information," Tiffany said. Mr. Hofstrom had fallen through to the Otherside when he was a teenager and knew a lot about the monsters that lived in that world. He was their best bet to figure out why everyone who ate the cookies was having weird dreams and was so sleepy during the daytime. Not to mention the bites.

Actually, Tiffany didn't really want to think about the bites. It made her feel queasy remembering the way Mason's arm looked.

Jeff used his mom's key to unlock the door. Once the door was open, the bakery loomed beyond, dark and forbidding.

"You go first," Evie said, her eyes large and round in her face.

Tiffany reached into her pocket and pulled out a flashlight. "I got this," Tiffany said. This was all her fault, anyway. If she hadn't taken the cookies to the sale, no one would've eaten them. If something happened to the people of Devils' Pass, Tiffany would never forgive herself. As a member of the Loyal Order of Helga, she was supposed to help people in her town — not put them directly into harm's way.

Inside the bakery, dust coated Tiffany's nose and made her sneeze. The flashlight illuminated bakery equipment covered in plastic, but that had the look of disuse.

Jeff came up next to Tiffany, holding his phone up like a flashlight. Pans were still sitting on metal preparation tables, and in one of the large mixers, leftover batter was growing fuzz. "Whoa, this place looks like everyone just ran out in the middle of work. What would make people do that?"

"Yeah. That's really weird. Let's check out the front," Tiffany said.

"You'd better turn off your flashlight. You don't want people to see the light from the street," Zach said. "Otherwise, goodbye stealth."

There was a loud click and the lights above came on, illuminating the space. Everyone turned around to look at Evie, who gave them a sheepish smile. "Whoops, I didn't know we were trying to be stealthy."

Tiffany laughed, but when she turned around, the laugh died in her throat. "Whoa, are you guys seeing this?" There was a thick layer of flour in the back room as though someone had dropped a bag and never cleaned it up. Crisscrossing the dust were hundreds of tiny footprints.

"Are those rat tracks?" Jeff asked.

"Oh, ick," Zach said, taking a dancing step toward the door outside.

Tiffany bent down, shaking her head. "No, look. The spacing is all wrong. It's like tiny little people tracks."

The group fell silent as they considered what could make such strange tracks.

A moan came from behind one of the large mixing machines, and everyone jumped.

"Did you hear that?" Tiffany whispered.

"We should get out of here," Evie said.

"Not until we find out what that noise was," Tiffany said.

"I didn't hear anything," Zach said.

They heard the muffled noise again. It was louder this time and unmistakable. It sounded like someone moaning in pain.

They were not alone in the bakery.

CHAPTER ELEVEN

Things Just Got Real

Tiffany began to tiptoe toward the sound. She knew it was a bad idea. After all, this was how people ended up getting eaten in scary movies. But the sound wouldn't stop, and Tiffany had to know what it was.

Evie stood back, her hands over her mouth and her eyes wide. Jeff and Zach followed Tiffany, hanging back just enough to run away if necessary. Their feet made the dust in the bakery rise and swirl, and Zach sneezed loudly.

Everyone froze.

The sound of muffled yelling became screaming, like someone had a gag over her mouth and was trying to yell for help. Something skittered from behind the mixing machines, keeping to the shadows and running along the wall.

"A rat!" Zach yelled.

Evie screamed and ran out of the building.

"I got her," Jeff said, following right behind her, his crutches loud in his hurry. Only Zach stayed behind. Tiffany's eyes met his.

"I don't think that was a rat," she said.

She moved toward the space that the small, scurrying creature had come from. The noises had stopped, but that didn't mean there wasn't anything to see behind the industrial mixer.

Behind the metal machine, wrapped in webbing that sparkled, was Mrs. Briggs.

Mrs. Briggs was wrapped up in a gray material that looked like dryer lint with a lot of sparkles mixed in. Her large form was completely cocooned in it, with

only her face sticking out. She moved back and forth like she was trying to get free, and her wide eyes landed on Zach and Tiffany.

"Mgbaskfjjklsofff," she said.

Her face had been bitten by some sort of small creature, the wounds looking similar to those on Mason's arm. The bite marks covered half her face and some of them looked fresh.

"We have to help her," Zach said.

Zach ran to the woman and began to tear away the sticky webbing. Tiffany held the flashlight as he got her free, her heart pounding in her throat. She'd been right about cookie monsters, but now, seeing Mrs. Briggs, she wished she hadn't been.

"Help . . . me," Mrs. Briggs rasped out, reaching her arms up to Zach.

Zach grabbed her arm. "We need to get out of here. NOW!" he said, pulling her from the bakery. Tiffany didn't argue. She grabbed Mrs. Briggs' other arm and the three of them ran awkwardly to the door.

A few feet from the door, Tiffany stopped and let go of Mrs. Briggs, letting Zach support her. She walked over to a shelf. Stacked on top of it were the trays the Cookie Lady had carried. And on top of that was a thick layer of what looked like dryer lint, fluffy and gray with just a hint of sparkle.

Just like the fluff wrapped around Mrs. Briggs.

"Hey, Tiff, what are you waiting for?" Zach called from outside.

She ran outside. Jeff was already calling 911 while Zach helped Mrs. Briggs lie down on the ground and get comfortable. Evie cried softly, and Tiffany went over to her and put her arm around her.

"Mrs. Briggs didn't sell her bakery," Tiffany said in a low voice to her friends after the ambulance finally arrived. They stood in front of the yarn shop across the street from the bakery and watched as Mrs. Briggs was loaded into the vehicle.

Like her face, Mrs. Briggs' arms had been chewed up as well. Red, angry bite marks covered both of her forearms. Whatever monster had been keeping her had also kept her wounds from getting infected, since there didn't seem to be any pus. Tiffany had studied up on types of infections, and there was no way an open wound like that could stay uninfected unless the creature's saliva had played some part.

"We need to find out what did this," Evie sniffled. Jeff pulled his sister into his side and gave her a hug. Zach stood off a little to the side and rubbed the back of his neck.

"We need to stop this before someone else gets hurt," Tiffany agreed.

CHAPTER TWELVE
Too Late

When Tiffany finally got home, she was starving. Her sister, Simone, was sitting in the living room watching television, and when Tiffany walked in, Simone looked up with an arched eyebrow.

"Grandma know you were out and about?" she asked.

"I had study group," Tiffany answered. It wasn't exactly a lie. After all, they were investigating what was going on with the bakery. It was a little bit like studying, discovering new facts and all that.

Tiffany tried to put the memory of Mrs. Briggs out of her head. Remembering how Mrs. Briggs had been chewed on by some monster made it hard to keep her appetite . . .

Tiffany walked into the kitchen and rummaged through the pantry. "Hey, what happened to the Veggie Crisps?"

"I ate them," Simone called from the living room. "But I think there are some cookies left over from the bakery that just went out of business."

Tiffany froze. "Did you eat them?"

Simone laughed. "No, weirdo. I told you, I have the meet against Hilderbrand Prep next month. You know I don't eat junk food during the cross-country season. Grandma saved them for you. They had raisins in them. She hates raisins, but knows you like them."

Tiffany went to the cupboard and searched for the cookies. She had to get rid of them before her grandma or sister ate them. It was bad enough that most of Devils' Pass was suffering from the sleep sickness and weird bites, but now people's faces were being chewed off. Things were getting decidedly worse.

The package of cookies had fallen down behind a couple of jars of pasta sauce. Tiffany picked it up and let out a yelp.

"Are you OK?" Simone called from the living room.

"Yeah, fine, just almost dropped something." The bag Tiffany held was clear cellophane and the Cookies and More logo was on the front of the bag. But inside there weren't any cookies — just a huge pile of fluffy dryer lint and glitter with a few raisins at the bottom.

"What the heck?" Tiffany muttered. It looked exactly like the stuff back in the bakery. But what was it? She definitely didn't want to touch it.

Tiffany put the bag inside another sandwich bag and then put that bag inside a paper bag. She had to get in touch with Mr. Hofstrom. He would know what it was.

"Hey," Simone called from the living room. "Doesn't this kid go to school with you?"

Tiffany ran into the living room, the paper bag full of nastiness still clutched in her hand. On TV was a shot of the Briggs' house, with several people being rolled out the front door, all on stretchers.

"Turn it up," Tiffany said. Simone pushed the button on the remote and the newscaster's voice filled the living room.

"An entire family has been devoured in a tragedy authorities are blaming on rabid squirrels. Earlier this evening, forty-three-year-old Emmaline Briggs was found in the back room of her bakery suffering from multiple bite wounds," the newscaster said. The TV showed a picture of Mrs. Briggs being brought out of the bakery on a stretcher. Tiffany cringed when she saw Mrs. Briggs' face again.

The newscaster said, "Authorities arrived at the home of Emmaline Briggs to notify her family that she'd been in an accident. Once there, police found four additional victims: forty-four-year-old Jason Briggs, seventeen-year-old Betsy Briggs, and fourteen-year-old Mason Briggs. All of them have been hospitalized and are reported to be in stable condition.

"Fifty-six-year-old Mary Rogers of Dunsville, who has been missing for several weeks, was also at the house and was found dead when they arrived at the scene. All four victims suffered from bite wounds and were tied up when officers arrived. They shared the same pattern of bite marks as the victim found in the bakery."

"Sure are a lot of animal attacks in this town," Simone muttered. "I can't believe squirrels could do that."

Tiffany watched the news with a clenched fist. Mary Rogers was the Cookie Lady, and now she was dead.

Time to stop these monsters, and fast.

CHAPTER THIRTEEN
Fancy Meeting You Here

Tiffany tried calling Mr. Hofstrom for an hour. She tried dialing the library's number and then she tried instant messaging. She'd even sent him a dozen emails with pictures of the glitter fluff, even though she kept it in the bag and was careful not to touch it. But he didn't respond to any of it.

She worried that maybe Mr. Hofstrom had eaten the cookies as well. He never left the library. No one knew whether it was because he was afraid to or because he was cursed — he refused to talk about it.

But that didn't mean someone couldn't have brought him cookies to eat.

What if he was alone and sleepless this very minute, a small creature wrapping him up in glitter fluff to feed on him?

Tiffany shook her head. No, Mr. Hofstrom was fine. He had survived the Otherside. He could survive cookie monsters.

There was nothing Tiffany could do until the morning, so she put her frantic thoughts aside and went to sleep.

A good time later, Tiffany looked at her alarm clock and sighed. It was nearly midnight, but she couldn't sleep. Her head was full of questions about the gross — and somehow deadly — cookies. Why had they given everyone nightmares? Were they the ploy of some kind of nightmare creature? Or maybe something they'd never fought before? But if the creature was tied to nightmares, why had it covered people in that weird fluff and eaten them? Those seemed like two different goals.

Tiffany kicked off her covers and got out of bed. Maybe a snack would help her sleep. When she was little, her mom used to make her a cream cheese and jam sandwich when she couldn't sleep. Her mom had been dead for a few years. Like Jeff, she'd had cancer, but she hadn't survived hers. After that, cream cheese and jam sandwiches were Tiffany's favorite even more.

They only sometimes made her sad.

Tiffany put on her slippers and padded downstairs to the kitchen. She didn't bother turning on the kitchen light because she didn't want to wake Simone or her grandma. By the light of the fridge, Tiffany got out the strawberry jam, bread, and the fluffy cream cheese she loved. She'd just assembled her sandwich and was getting ready to take a big bite when she looked out the window and froze.

Was that Zach shuffling down the middle of the street?

It was! He wore pajama pants and just a T-shirt. It was way too cold out for that.

Why was he outside?

Tiffany put down her sandwich and slipped on her jacket and some shoes. She ran out the front door and after Zach. It was late, so she didn't want to yell at him. Instead, she waited until she was right next to him before trying to shake him awake.

"Zach, Zach! You're sleepwalking!" Zach didn't say anything. He just kept walking, oblivious to the cold and his bare feet on the road.

Tiffany began to worry. Had Zach always sleepwalked or was this because of the cookies? She'd read once that you weren't supposed to wake a sleepwalker — that they should wake up on their own. But she didn't have time for that. She had to wake him up. Only she didn't have anything to wake him up with.

Maybe a cold shower?

Tiffany ran home and grabbed a cup from the cupboard. She filled it with cold water and ran back out the door. But when she got outside, there was no one around.

Where had Zach gone?

Tiffany ran in the direction she'd last seen him. She spotted him again when she got to the end of the block, heading toward Main Street. Tiffany ran after him, water sloshing over the sides of the cup. As soon as she was close, she threw the water all over him, hoping it was enough to wake him up.

"Gah, what, stop!" Zach threw his hands up to ward off any more water.

"Oh, thank goodness." Tiffany bent over and took a deep breath. "I was afraid it wouldn't work."

Zach blinked and looked around. "Wait! How did I get here? What am I doing out of bed?" Zach crossed his arms and started to shiver. "Oh, man, it is cold out."

"Let's go to my house. I'll grab you a towel and you can dry off."

They made their way back to Tiffany's house, and while they walked, Tiffany couldn't help but say, "So, this is kind of weird, right?"

Zach laughed. "Yeah, just a little."

"Have you ever sleepwalked? Did you do that in L.A. before you moved here?"

Zach shook his head and gave a shiver. "No, no way. I never have. You?"

Tiffany grinned and shrugged. "Not me. Well, I mean, we did have that time when nightmares were stalking people's dreams. But mostly people just kept waking up covered in mud and horsehair."

Zach's widened. "You're joking, right?"

Tiffany shook her head. "Nope. Thank goodness Mr. Hofstrom knew what was happening. I had to sneak cups of coffee into my room for a week before we'd finally banished them all. Nightmares love coffee: you have to pretend you're asleep, wait until they're drinking the coffee, and then you shoot the nightmare with milk or half and half."

"Now I know you're teasing me," Zach said. But after a beat, he added, "What do they look like?"

"Like the doom unicorns, but made of black smoke." Tiffany laughed. "Apparently a glass of milk really is the only thing you need to get rid of nightmares." They chuckled quietly.

"OK, we should keep our voices down, everyone is asleep. I'll go grab a towel."

She ran to the bathroom and grabbed a towel. When she came back out, Zach was sitting in the living room, talking with her grandma.

"Grandma! I'm sorry. I was trying not to wake you up." Embarrassment heated Tiffany's cheeks. It looked like she'd tried to sneak a boy into her grandma's house, and even though Zach was a boy, it wasn't like that at all.

"Tiffany, what is going on?" her grandma asked. "This young man said that you found him sleepwalking. That's very serious business. We need to call his mom."

Tiffany gnawed on her lower lip. "I was just going to help him dry off and then I figured I could walk him home."

"Not at this time of night. You don't know what kind of strange people are out and about."

Tiffany's grandma was even taller than Tiffany, over six feet tall, with dark skin, steel gray dreadlocks piled on top of her head, and a no-nonsense gaze. She was not the kind of woman you argued with.

"Yes, ma'am," Tiffany said, and handed Zach the towel. "Sorry."

Zach shrugged. "It could be worse. I was in the middle of the worst dream when you found me."

"Cookie dreams again?" Tiffany asked while her grandma dug in her purse for her cell phone.

Zach nodded. "I thought you were being silly when you said the cookies were causing everyone to be tired. But now I think you might be right."

Tiffany sat back on the couch. Now that they knew the cookies were causing the trouble and making everyone sleepy, what about the people being eaten? How were the two connected?

Tiffany knew it was time to find out.

CHAPTER FOURTEEN

Hair's the Deal...

The next day after school, Evie and Tiffany walked to the library. Tiffany had stopped by before school too, but no amount of knocking and ringing the bell could summon Mr. Hofstrom. She'd finally headed to school, sick with worry and guilt.

If she'd somehow contributed to something bad happening to Mr. Hofstrom, she would never forgive herself.

The bag of weird gray fluff had been in Tiffany's locker all day, and just knowing it was near all of her books and other things made her feel grossed out. The sooner she could get rid of it, and maybe get some answers, the better.

The library was empty of users when they walked in, but Mr. Hofstrom sat behind the circulation desk. He wore a blue tracksuit and a gold chain, the metal bright against his dark skin. He might not seem like the typical librarian type, but he was really smart.

"Tiffany, Evie! How're you girls doing today?" Mr. Hofstrom asked. He was listening to music from the eighties. He'd been in high school when he'd gone through to the Otherside, and when he came back twenty years later, he hadn't aged. He still liked to wear tracksuits and listen to the same music, and he looked far too young to run a library by himself.

"You're OK!" Tiffany said happily.

Mr. Hofstrom frowned. "Of course. Why?"

"I tried calling your cell phone and Face-timing you last night," Tiffany said.

Mr. Hofstrom gave Tiffany a sheepish grin. "Technology still freaks me out. I turned everything off.

I was watching my VHS of *Breakin' 2: Electric Boogaloo*. Best movie ever."

Evie cleared her throat. "We have a situation, Mr. Hofstrom," she said.

He sat up straight and leaned forward. "An Otherside problem?"

Tiffany reached into her backpack and pulled out the paper bag that held the fluff. "Always."

Mr. Hofstrom took the paper bag and looked in with an expression of trepidation on his face. "Oh no. Let's go into my office."

They followed Mr. Hofstrom to his office through a door that said EMPLOYEES ONLY. Since he couldn't go outside, Mr. Hofstrom lived in the basement of the library. His office was almost like a kitchen: refrigerator, microwave, cupboards filled with food. Everyone in the Loyal Order had tried to get it out of Mr. Hofstrom, why he couldn't go outside. But asking never yielded anything more than a polite smile and a change of subject.

Mr. Hofstrom pointed at one of the cupboards. "I have those granola bars you like, Tiffany."

She shook her head. "I don't have much of an appetite right now."

Evie's eyes widened. "Oh, man, you must be super worried."

"It's my fault everyone ate the cookies. If it hadn't been for my stupid cookie sale and me buying the cookies from that bakery, Mary Rogers would still be alive," Tiffany said, guilt welling up once more. "And the Briggses would be unharmed!" If only she hadn't burned her cookies! If only she hadn't used the clearly dangerous bakery cookies for the sale none of this would have happened.

"I highly doubt it. If this is what I think it is, there's no way any of this is your fault," Mr. Hofstrom said.

Evie frowned. "What do you think it is?"

He said, "It looks like elf hair."

"What?" Tiffany and Evie squealed at the same time.

Mr. Hofstrom went to his filing cabinet and pulled out the folder where he kept all of his notes on Otherside weirdness. It said "Trapper Keeper" on the side and had a red car on the cover, a totally cheesy eighties picture. But that folder had all the information about the Otherside that they needed.

He opened his folder and pulled out a piece of notebook paper with sketches. "Elves. Nasty little creatures. Usually between sixteen and twenty-two inches tall. Their hair is actually a type of fungus. Contact with it leaves victims susceptible to their control. Elves control people, make them do their work for them for a while, and then they eat them."

"Like the Briggs family," Evie said.

"The elves were at the bakery first?" Mr. H asked.

"Yes," Tiffany said. "We saw something that we thought was a rat there, but it looked weird."

"That was probably an elf. They don't like to be seen. They're totally disgusting," Mr. Hofstrom said. "I mean, they make people eat their hair."

Tiffany thought of the weird webbing around Mrs. Briggs and gagged. "Guh. Gross. The elves put their hair in the cookies? I think I'm going to be sick," she said, holding her stomach.

"Oh, no!" Evie clapped a hand over her mouth. "Jeff ate those cookies!"

Mr. Hofstrom shook his head. "Worse. Their hair ARE the cookies. Elves can weave their hair into different creations to attract their prey: cotton candy, berries, you name it, elves have done it. When I was on the Otherside, there was an apple tree that had the best apples. They weren't apples at all, though, but an elf trap."

Tiffany nodded, her brain working through the mechanics of it all. "But what does that have to do with people having nightmares and not sleeping? I mean, why would they make people sleepwalk?"

"Simple. The elves create a psychic link with their prey through their hair and then through their saliva. Once an elf begins feeding on someone, they can make them do whatever they want until the person dies."

Evie gasped. "The Cookie Lady! Mary Rogers from Dunsville. That must have been how she ended up at the Briggs' house."

Tiffany nodded and turned to Mr. Hofstrom. "The report said Mary Rogers went missing overnight."

He nodded. "That psychic link is strongest when a person is asleep. So it's easiest for them to control their victims then. Soon-to-be victims have nightmares and might get glimpses of what is happening within the elf den while they're asleep."

"Bad cookie dreams," Evie said.

"But sleepwalking?" Tiffany asked.

"If people are sleepwalking, it's because an elf is trying to summon them to their lair for dinner," Mr. Hofstrom said.

"So the reason I found Zach sleepwalking last night is because the elves wanted to eat him. Is that what you're saying?" Tiffany asked.

"Yup," Mr. Hofstrom said. "Zach is most definitely on the creeptastic elf menu."

Tiffany shuddered. If she hadn't been hungry so late the night before, Zach might have been something else's dinner.

"So how do we save everyone?" Evie asked.

Mr. Hofstrom closed the book and leaned against the filing cabinet. "You need to get rid of the elves, of course. Follow a few of their 'dinners' to the lair. Elves can be defeated by either fire or water. They're elemental creatures."

Evie said, "Oh, so if we find a way to light them on fire or douse them in water, they'll die?"

Mr. Hofstrom nodded.

"Let's hope water works," Tiffany said. "I don't want to light anything on fire."

"Maybe we can just nicely ask the elves to leave town?" Evie said with a hopeful smile. She was a pacifist and hated the idea of hurting any creature, even the monsters from the Otherside. But the look on Mr. Hofstrom's face stopped her smiling. She said, "Yeah, yeah." She knew there was no way around it.

"There's one thing I don't get, though," Tiffany said. "Why not eat everyone all at once? They only took small bites out of the Briggs family."

Mr. Hofstrom frowned. "They've been taking their time up to now because they didn't think anyone was on to them. But now that you've uncovered one of their lairs, they'll move faster. You're going to have to hurry to catch them before they eat everyone who is left."

"Oh, no!" Evie exclaimed. "Jeff and Zach could get eaten."

Tiffany sighed. "Thanks, Mr. Hofstrom." She tapped her fingers against her lips. Now that she knew what they were up against, she knew how they could fix this.

She looped her arm through Evie's and pulled her toward the door. "Come on, Evie. I think this calls for a sleepover."

CHAPTER FIFTEEN
The Hard Part

Tiffany was an expert at planning sleepovers. And she was pretty good at getting her grandma to change her mind when she told her no about something. But never had so much depended on spending the night over at Evie's house.

And it was not going well.

"I don't like the idea of you having a sleepover on a school night." Tiffany's grandma flipped through her magazine. They were standing in the kitchen, Evie hugging herself, while Tiffany tried every tactic she could think of.

"We're going to work on a school project." Not true.

"We'll be asleep by ten." Also not true.

"Evie's mom is totally OK with it." Not even close to being true, but since she was out of town, this was the tiniest fib Tiffany had told.

Tiffany's grandma kept flipping through her magazine. "What's really going on, Tiffany? Why don't you try for the truth now?"

Tiffany sighed and looked at Evie. This was always the tricky part about trying to save the town. No one thought kids could do something like that, and why should they? After all, adults had been underestimating kids since the beginning of time.

But more importantly, the town had goldfish memory. No one ever remembered the bad things that came from the sinkhole except for Mr. Hofstrom, sometimes the mayor, and Tiffany and her friends. In other words, just the Loyal Order of Helga remembered. She had some theories as to why that was, but mostly it just meant that they spent a lot of time fixing things and no one ever knew.

Seeing that lying hadn't gotten Tiffany permission to sleep over at Evie's house, she decided to try the truth. "Well, there are elves in town and they've psychically enslaved everyone who ate the cookies so that they can summon them when they want and then eat them. So we're going to spend the night at Evie's house and follow Jeff and Zach when they get up in the middle of the night to go become elf chow. And then we're going to either soak the elves or set them on fire, whichever one seems to destroy them."

Tiffany's grandma looked up from her magazine, looking from Evie and back to Tiffany. Tiffany took a deep breath. Was it possible that worked?

Her grandma snorted. And then she started laughing.

"OK, Tiffany, you obviously really want to go spend the night. Just make sure you really are asleep by ten. I know you've got that science test tomorrow."

Tiffany kissed her grandma on the cheek. "Thank you, Grandma. And no worries on the test. I'm totally going to ace it."

She and Evie ran to her room. "I cannot believe that worked," Evie said.

"Let's not celebrate too soon. We still have to save the town."

Evie nodded. "I know, but after convincing your grandma to let us have a sleepover on a school night, that seems almost easy."

Tiffany laughed.

CHAPTER SIXTEEN
Fitting In

At midnight, Tiffany opened her third Jazzy cola and yawned widely. Evie chewed a vegan gummy worm and sighed. They were both tired, but sleep was not an option if they wanted to save the town.

Next door in Jeff's room, he and Zach were snoring loudly enough to be heard through the wall. They'd all gone to bed by ten, just as Tiffany had promised her grandma. And while the boys had gone right to sleep, the girls had started on a caffeine and sugar regimen to keep themselves awake.

"What if the elves don't summon them tonight?" Evie asked.

Tiffany groaned. "Don't say that. Don't even suggest it or think about it."

Evie sighed. "Want to watch TV?"

"Might as well. As loud as the guys are, I'm sure we'll hear them."

Evie turned on the TV and they were halfway through a new episode of *Gem War Attack* when there was a thump from next door.

"Did you hear that?" Evie whispered.

The thump came again and the girls ran to the door, cracking it open to look into the hallway.

"Look," Evie whispered. Jeff and Zach were lurching down the hallway toward the front door. Jeff was wearing his prosthetic leg again.

"He hates wearing his prosthesis . . . ," Evie said.

"Huh, maybe the elves made him wear it?" Tiffany tapped her lips.

"I don't like these creepy elves," Evie muttered.

The girls slipped out of the room and followed the boys, staying a little way behind. They walked through downtown toward Main Street, past the bakery, and out to the middle school.

"Wait, are we going to the school?" Evie asked.

"Looks like it. Weird." Tiffany didn't like this at all.

Jeff and Zach weren't the only people walking toward the school. Principal Lopcz, Alicia Arnold and her dad, and most of the town were walking toward Devils' Pass Middle School.

"Let's try to blend in with the crowd," Tiffany suggested, and Evie nodded.

"I just hope we don't get eaten," she whispered.

The flow of people entered the hallway and then went down to the basement. Tiffany hadn't even known there was a basement in the middle school, and when they got down there, it took everything she had to hide her shock and pretend to be sleepwalking like everyone else.

There, in the basement, were big piles of the elf hair. It stood along the edges of the walls and in the corners, drifting up like dust bunnies.

"Don't touch the hair," Tiffany whispered.

"No way," Evie said.

All of the people were moving toward the hair. Tiffany looked around the room. Toward the back there were big boxes with the Cookies and More logo on the side. Tiffany pointed them out to Evie.

"I think the elves are going global," she said. "They're going to ship their cookies all over the world so they can eat lots of different people."

"We have to stop them," Evie said, a quiver in her voice.

Tiffany nodded.

Everyone stopped, and from the back of the room came a scratching sound, like a herd of rats.

"Iznik! Biz nie kleep groot," a voice squeaked.

Tiffany went still, and next to her Evie began to shake.

The elves had arrived.

CHAPTER SEVENTEEN

Worst Dinner Party Ever

Tiffany didn't want to move too much. All around her, the people enslaved by the cookie elves stood very still. But she also wanted to see what these elves looked like. She'd seen the footprints in the bakery, tiny little footprints that looked incredibly human. And they could talk, because she could hear them chirping back and forth at each other in tiny voices as they walked toward the boxes. So maybe they were just like tiny people?

Tiffany leaned back a little to look past the row of people standing to either side of her. She could see the elves at the front of the room.

They were hideous.

They were small, only slightly taller than a roll of paper towels. They wore strange little uniforms and their tiny bodies were a sickly gray. Their heads were strangely flat, and they had large, pointed ears and beady black eyes. Their stomachs were wide and round, their arms and legs skinny, and the weird hair grew all over in odd patches.

Two of the elves were talking to each other, standing right behind Alicia Arnold. She wore sleep shorts, and one of the elves opened its mouth, its black tongue coming out to lick her bare leg, saliva dripping from needle-sharp teeth.

The other elf screamed and attacked the elf who had licked Alicia. As they fought one another, a slightly taller elf came over, hitting both of them. The two smaller elves ducked their heads.

"That must be the boss elf," Tiffany murmured to Evie, nodding toward the big elf walking up and down the line.

"Oh, god, those things are so gross," Evie muttered. "What's the plan?"

Tiffany looked around. "Well, fire is a really bad idea. I don't want to burn the school down. And when I threw water on Zach, he woke up. So maybe we find a way to trigger the sprinklers and hope it melts the elves."

"Fingers crossed," Evie murmured.

The boss elf yelled out, "Kripnik plut!" and all the people on either side of them knelt before the piles of elf hair.

Everyone but Tiffany and Evie.

"Crap," Tiffany said. The elves were all looking at them, their beady eyes narrowed.

"You think they noticed?" Evie whispered.

The elves began to walk toward them, teeth bared, weird chirping noises coming from the back of their throats.

"Oh yeah." Tiffany said. "Look over there."
She pointed to the fire hose toward the back of the

basement. "See if you can get that working. I'll hold them off."

"Good luck!" Evie ran toward the fire hose, and Tiffany turned toward the elves.

"Let's go, creepers," Tiffany said, even though she was more afraid than she'd ever been.

The elves rushed at her. Tiffany kicked the first one, sending it sailing into the ceiling before it hit the ground hard, bouncing off the concrete floor. The other elves hung back, reluctant to meet the same fate as their friend.

"Tiffany, it's stuck!" Evie called.

Tiffany turned around to see what she was talking about.

And that's when the elves attacked.

CHAPTER EIGHTEEN
Practice Makes Perfect

The elves swarmed Tiffany's legs, hanging on to her jeans and climbing her like she was some kind of mountain. She yelped and tried to shake them off, but they were determined. A few had begun biting her with their gross teeth, ripping through the material of her jeans. One even managed to break through to the skin. Tiffany expected it to hurt, but instead the elf teeth were just really, really cold and made her skin feel numb.

That scared her more than anything else.

Tiffany jumped up and down, trying to dislodge the elves. She didn't want to touch them because they were covered with that weird hair, and she had the feeling that touching it would make her zombified like everyone else.

"Evie, hurry up!" Tiffany yelled, shaking an elf off her pant leg and kicking it across the room.

But when she turned around, Evie was nowhere near the fire hose. Instead, she was kneeling next to the pile of elf hair just like everyone else.

The elves had gotten to her.

Tiffany kicked another elf away from her and ran toward the fire hose. The elves followed, chirping and gurgling at her. One got in front of her foot and she stepped on it. It exploded like stomping on a snail would, a crunching followed by a gush of sparkling slime. Tiffany tasted Jazzy cola in the back of her throat but she didn't have time to throw up.

She had to save her friends and the town. If she got turned like the rest of them, Devils' Pass would be lost.

Tiffany kicked the last elf to the side and reached the fire hose. But now she understood why Evie hadn't been able to use it. The fire hose had an OUT OF ORDER sign on it.

"In case of emergency, pull sprinkler release," Tiffany read. "Great, where's that?"

Tiffany looked around the basement. There, next to the boiler, was the sprinkler release.

And about thirty elves stood between her and the button.

Tiffany took a deep breath. She needed to clear the elves out of the way without touching them. Already, elf hair clung to her pant legs, and she was pretty sure that just one touch of the hair would make her enslaved along with everyone else. She needed to do something right now.

She looked around frantically. The elves were closing in on her, some of them baring their teeth. Finally, an idea struck her. In the corner of the basement was a box of old soccer balls. She grabbed one and dropped it on the ground. It was a little flat, but it would have to do.

Finally time to practice for next month's soccer tryouts, she thought to herself, smiling a little.

But this time, she had to keep flawless control of the ball.

She took a deep breath and closed her eyes, then opened them. "Let's do this," she said. She used the inside of her foot to control the ball, and dribbled it between the rows of people, using the ball to knock the elves to the side.

The elves started to run, but Tiffany was relentless. With perfect control, she managed to knock elves away left and right. She was almost to the sprinkler valve when a soft weight dropped onto her from above.

"Flirgerbergity cha!"

The boss elf had just landed on Tiffany's head.

Tiffany squealed. There was no more time to be clever. She kicked the ball into a group of the elves, and then ran as fast as she could across the room. The elf on her head gibbered and dug its fingers into her hair to hold on.

Tiffany ran across the room and punched the red emergency button. At first nothing happened, and Tiffany was worried that she'd been wrong. What if the button wasn't for the sprinklers?

But it didn't matter because Tiffany was starting to feel really relaxed.

Like, super duper awesome.

She yawned. Simone was right. She was an overachiever. She didn't have to do anything but sit next to those piles of delicious cookies — not hair, but delicious, delicious cookies — and put them in boxes.

It seemed like such a great idea. The only idea, really.

Just as she began to kneel down near the boxes, a fire alarm sounded. Water rained down, and the elves screamed. They ran, some of them trying to hide under the boiler and old gym equipment. The water was everywhere, though, and the elves had nowhere to go.

The boss elf jumped off of Tiffany's head and tried to run for the door. Halfway there, he began to shrink. He got smaller and smaller until he was nothing but a gray pebble. The other elves changed into pebbles as well, and the loopy feeling that had threatened to overtake Tiffany lifted. She let out a huge sigh of relief.

The gray, floofy elf hair melted down like cotton candy and began to gather in murky puddles. The people of Devils' Pass began to wake up, confused and yawning widely.

Zach's mom — Principal Lopez — stood in the middle of the room wearing a Devils' Pass Middle School T-shirt and sleep shorts. She took charge immediately.

"Everyone, please file out calmly. This way, this way!" she said as she walked to the staircase out of the basement. People followed her, muttering all the way, some raking their hands through their hair. Everyone looked baffled.

Evie came up to Tiffany. "You did it!" she said, grabbing her arm and jumping up and down.

"Yep." Tiffany beamed, feeling pretty good. "And I think I might make the soccer team! But let's get out of here. I'm sure someone is going to start asking questions, and I do not want to be around when that starts happening."

As if on cue, Alicia Arnold asked, "How did we all end up here?" Her teeth chattered as they walked through the cold night air.

"Overnight lock-in fundraiser," Evie said with a grin. "But it looks like we won't get to bake cookies after all," she said.

Tiffany groaned and grinned back.

CHAPTER NINETEEN
A Good Night's Sleep

After everyone had gotten out of the building, the fire trucks arrived. No one could quite explain what they'd been doing in the basement of the school. Even if they were at a lock-in fundraiser, it would've been held in the cafeteria or the gym, not a dank basement. But since no one was hurt very badly, everyone just seemed to let it go. The firefighters sent everyone home. They were busy, and a few weirdos who were dripping and confused but relatively unscathed were not their problem. After all, there was a rabid squirrel problem that still needed to be dealt with.

Zach, Jeff, Evie, and Tiffany walked toward home, huddled together and shivering. The firefighters had given them blankets but they were still soaked, and the cold night air was not helping. Now that the elves had been stopped, the sleepover was totally unnecessary. Both Zach and Jeff were quiet while Evie and Tiffany chattered, still wired on caffeine and sugar.

"Oh, man, when that giant elf fell on your head, I thought it was over," Evie said.

"You saw that?"

"Yeah. It was weird, like I couldn't do what I wanted, but I could still tell what was going on. Thank goodness the water melted those things. They were super creepy."

"And yet, Alicia Arnold didn't remember anything," Zach said. "Neither did my mom."

"Do you?" Tiffany asked.

"Oh yeah, I remember everything," Zach said.

"Of course he does. The power of the Loyal Order of Helga strikes again," Jeff said.

"Hey, how do you think they got here?" Zach asked.

Tiffany frowned. "What do you mean?"

"They had to come through the sinkhole, right? So, how did they get through the water from the Otherside to here without melting?"

Everyone fell silent, contemplating the possibilities. "Maybe they built a ship, like a spaceship," Jeff said.

"Maybe they had magic of some kind," Evie said.

"Or maybe they didn't come through the sinkhole at all," Tiffany said.

"What do you mean?" Zach asked.

"Maybe the sinkhole isn't the only doorway to the Otherside. Maybe there are more," Tiffany said. "What if there are all kinds of doorways to the Otherside in Devils' Pass?"

"Oh, man," Evie said, wrapping her arms around herself. "Just think of all the stuff that could maybe get through."

They walked home the rest of the way in silence, and if they all had trouble sleeping that night it wasn't because of the elves and their cookies. Not one bit.

COOKIE ELVES

Origin: *Otherside*

Colors: *gray, multi-color hair*

Likes: *eating humans; cookies; minions*

Dislikes: *Water. Water will defeat them.*

Note on hair: Their hair can be molded into anything. It gives off an odor and taste pleasing to humans.

CLOSE UP
OF
HAIR FUNGUS

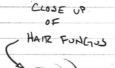

This creature is usually found in bakeries, especially in small towns. Cookie elves are between sixteen and twenty four inches tall with mottled gray bumpy skin similar to a toad's. These creatures have hair that is made of a fungus that resembles dryer lint. They spin their hair into cookies to lure in their victims.

Unlike cake elves, cookie elves often use their prey as mindless servants prior to eating them. They can also be destroyed by using the opposite of their element.

Note: The encountered cookie elves were destroyed with water. I believe that these cookie elves did not come through the sinkhole in Devils' Pass. Reach out to other librarians to see if they have also seen these elves.

HATES
FIRE
&
WATER

H^2O

GLOSSARY

askew–not straight; tilted

dank–musty and damp

delusion–something that isn't real, but feels real

douse–to pour liquid over

foiled–stopped

oblivious–not paying attention; unaware

pacifist–someone who wants peace

queasy–the feeling of an upset stomach

regimen–routine

robocall–an automated call where the caller is a recorded message

skitter–to move quickly and in a jerky way

susceptible–easily impressionable or unresistant

unorthodox–unusual or unconventional

YOU SHOULD TALK

1. Tiffany is involved with many different types of activities. Talk about how this helps and/or hinders Tiffany when it comes to fighting monsters.

2. Tiffany says that finding Zach sleepwalking outside was a coincidence. Do you think this is true? Knowing Devils' Pass, are there other things it could be? Use the text to explain your answer.

3. Have you ever had to convince your parents or guardians that you needed to have a sleepover? What arguments did you use?

WRITE ON

1. Tiffany has to leave in the middle of the night to go save the town. Write a note that she might have left for her grandmother in case she woke up.

2. Write an entry in Mr. Hofstrom's Trapper Keeper about the elves. What would you include and how would you organize the information?

3. Pretend you're a newspaper reporter. Write an article about the mysterious case of the Briggses.

ABOUT THE AUTHOR

Justina Ireland lives with her husband, kid, and dog in Pennsylvania. She is the author of *Vengeance Bound* and *Promise of Shadows*, both from Simon and Schuster Books for Young Readers. Her forthcoming young adult book *Dread Nation* will be available in 2018 from HarperCollins and her adult debut *The Never and the Now* will be available from Tor/Macmillan. You can find Justina on Twitter as @justinaireland or visit her website, justinaireland.com.

ABOUT THE ILLUSTRATOR

Tyler Champion is a freelance illustrator and designer. He grew up in Kentucky before moving to New Jersey to develop his passion at The Joe Kubert School of Cartoon and Graphic Art. After graduating in 2010 he headed back south to Nashville, Tennessee, where he currently resides with his girlfriend and soon-to-be first kiddo. He has produced work for magazines, comics, design companies, and now children's books; including work for Sony Music, F(r)iction magazine, Paradigm games, and Tell-A-Graphics. You can see more of his work at tylerchampionart.com.